To Sailor,
Merry Christmas!
2020
Love,
NamaJen &
Grampa

This book belongs to ~~████~~

CYRIL

In the humid depths of the
Costa Rican rainforest

Lived a sloth called Cyril
and his big brother Horace.

Horace was content and never felt bored,
but Cyril was restless and his mind always soared...

...With dreams of adventure,
Leaving the jungle behind
With his sights on the city
where life was refined.

With all of his belongings
Cyril caught a small plane,

which flew out of the forest
that glistened with rain.

Over the mountains and
rivers so pretty,

Cyril could not wait
to explore the big city.

First stop was a restaurant,
with food à la carte,

But poor slow Cyril
barely had time to start.

Toot
Toot Beep Honk
Honk....

...the cars sounded so angry,
when he crossed at the crossing
still feeling quite hungry.

Climbing frame,
some swings,
this place looks
like fun,

But so slowly
he climbed
that the kids
got SO glum.

Sprinkles and sauce
on Cyril's ice cream,

Which before he could eat it,
dripped off like a milk stream.

It was all so fast in
this place far from home,

Cyril slumped on a
bench and felt so alone.

He looked up through his tears and saw a great sight,

A picture of home and a very cheap flight!

As fast as he could,
which was really quite slow
Cyril gathered his things
and decided to go...

Back home to Horace
and his home in the jungle,
where time passed quite
slowly and nobody grumbled.

He realised then that
though adventure was nice,
being back home
was just paradise.